The Animals Would Not Sleep!

Sara Levine

Illustrated by **Marta Álvarez Miguéns**

ini **Charlesbridge**

The animals were making a ruckus.

"It's getting close to bedtime," Marco's mom said. "Time to put away your toys."

"You mean time to sort the animals," Marco said.
"That's what a scientist would do."

Flying
Animals

Marco made signs for his baskets.

He put each animal where it belonged.

But the animals would not go to sleep.

Fly!

Flying Animals

Swim!

Slither!

They egged one another on until
not one remained in its container.

Leap!

Swimming
Animals

Animals
Move on

Crawl!

Perhaps they just weren't tired enough yet. Marco gave them a little more time to get their wild out.

"Marco," his mom called. "Almost ready?"
"Umm, almost," Marco called back.

Marco studied his menagerie, as a
good scientist would. Maybe the
animals would have better behavior
if they were organized differently.

He made new signs and tucked the animals in their appropriate baskets.

Mostly Brown

Black and White

Colors of the
Rainbow

But Zebra was upset. While he didn't mind sleeping next to Stingray and Kingsnake, he missed his friend Giraffe. He started crying.

Marco felt terrible. "You're probably just overtired now—that's why it seems like such a big deal," he told Zebra.

He dumped all the animals out. Maybe he should group them by size, so medium-sized Zebra and medium-sized Giraffe could be together.

It was hard to fit the large ones into their basket, but Marco squeezed them all in.

He started to put his pajamas on. But he didn't get far—a terrible sound was coming from the basket labeled *Large*.

Marco peered inside.

"I'm smooshed," Dinosaur said. "My spikes are bent. I'll never fall asleep."

AAAAAAA!

"Me neither," said Dancing Flamingo. "My neck is cramped."

It did look uncomfortable.

"Plus, I miss Rainbow Bear," Dancing Flamingo added.

"What's going on in here?" Marco's mother asked. "Are you getting ready for bed?"

"I'm trying," Marco said, "but my animals aren't cooperating."

Now he heard squeaking and buzzing from the *Small* animal bin.

"What's going on in there?" Marco asked.

"Baby Mouse wants his mommy," Spotted Dotty explained.

"Also, it's too cold for us in this big, drafty basket," Turtle added.

"Two more minutes," Marco's mother called.

Marco had to think fast. Being a scientist, he was used to coming up with ideas and thinking outside the box. He dumped the animals back onto the floor.

"Can't I just sleep in your bed tonight?" whined Birthday Bear.

Yellow Bear started crying for no reason at all. Everyone was getting cranky, and time was running out.

Marco knew that good scientists care about their animals. Helping them feel safe and cozy was important. He also knew that sorting could still work.

He placed the large animals at the foot of his bed, where there was plenty of room to stretch out.

He placed the medium animals along the wall.

And he placed the small animals behind his pillows, where they would feel snug and warm.

He leaped into bed just in time.

Everything was quiet and still when
his mother came in to say good night.

"Good night, Mama," Marco said.

"Sleep tight, Marco," said his mom. "Looks
like you got everyone sorted and settled in."

"Yeah, well, that's what a scientist can do!"

Sorting in Science

Like Marco, scientists sort, or classify, animals by their characteristics. They divide animals into two groups: those with bones (or an internal skeleton of cartilage), called **vertebrates**, and those without bones, called **invertebrates**.

Vertebrates are divided into five main classes:

Mammals have hair or fur and make milk for their young.

Amphibians have soft eggs and slimy skin.

Birds have feathers.

Fish have fins and gills and spend their whole lives in the water.

Reptiles have scaly skin and eggs with hard shells.

Invertebrates are also divided into classes. Marco has animals from two of those classes:

Mollusks, such as snails and octopuses, have soft bodies with or without shells.

Arthropods, such as insects and crabs, have an exoskeleton (hard covering) and legs with joints.

Marco will learn about scientific classification when he gets older—but he already knows the most important thing about animals: caring for them requires both intelligence and empathy.

—Sara Levine, DVM

Former assistant professor of biology at Wheelock College

Exploring the Math

Marco wants to organize his animals so they are comfortable at bedtime. He first sorts them by how they move. He then sorts by color and size. Different ways of sorting yield different results. When he sorts by color, friends Zebra and Giraffe are tearfully separated. When he re-sorts by size, they are reunited. In the end Marco finds a solution that works for everyone.

As children explore sorting, they are thinking mathematically. They learn that they can sort sets—or organize data—in different ways. They also discover that the way they choose to sort matters.

Try this!

✳ **As children sort toys, ask them how they decide what goes where.** "How did you decide where to put the turtle?" "Why did you put this car with the rabbits?" There are many ways to sort—perhaps the car is with the rabbits in case they need a ride.

✳ **Invite children to find objects that share an attribute.** If you're on a walk, point out, "This leaf is the same size as your hand! Let's look for another leaf the same size."

✳ **Help children notice different features of objects.** Play the "three word" game. First pick an object you see—a toy, say. Ask children to describe it in three words. Then it's your turn: describe the same toy in three different words.

✳ **Encourage children to help you sort clean laundry.** Sort by family member and then by type of clothing. Then ask children to pick another way to sort—by color, for instance.

As children talk about sorting, they are using math to explore the world around them. Encourage them to think creatively, too—like Marco!

—**Karen Economopoulos**
Co-Director of the Investigations Center for Curriculum and Professional Development, TERC

Visit **www.charlesbridge.com/storytellingmath** for more activities.

For Dorothy—S. L.

For all young readers with an insatiable curiosity about how the world works—M. Á. M.

This book is supported in part by TERC under a grant from the Heising-Simons Foundation.

At the time of publication, all URLs printed in this book were accurate and active. Charlesbridge, TERC, the author, and the illustrator are not responsible for the content or accessibility of any website.

Developed in conjunction with TERC
2067 Massachusetts Avenue
Cambridge, MA 02140
(617) 873-9600
www.terc.edu

Published by Charlesbridge
9 Galen Street
Watertown, MA 02472
(617) 926-0329
www.charlesbridge.com

Printed in China
(hc) 10 9 8 7 6 5 4 3 2 1
(pb) 10 9 8 7 6 5 4 3 2 1

Library of Congress Cataloging-in-Publication Data
Names: Levine, Sara, author. | Álvarez Miguéns, Marta, 1976– illustrator.
Title: The animals would not sleep! / Sara Levine ; illustrated by Marta Álvarez Miguéns.
Description: Watertown, MA : Charlesbridge Publishing, [2020] | Series: Storytelling Math | Summary: "It is almost bedtime, but first young Marco must put away his collection of stuffed animal toys. As a budding scientist Marco tries different ways of sorting the animals, but the animals have their own ideas. Marco scrambles to make everyone happy and make it to bed before his mother comes to tuck him in."—Provided by publisher
Identifiers: LCCN 2019027461 (print) | LCCN 2019027462 (ebook) | ISBN 9781623541286 (hardcover) | ISBN 9781623541972 (paperback) | ISBN 9781632899057 (ebook)
Subjects: LCSH: Soft toys—Juvenile fiction. | Imagination—Juvenile fiction. | Bedtime—Juvenile fiction. | Mothers and sons—Juvenile fiction. | CYAC: Toys—Fiction. | Imagination—Fiction. | Bedtime—Fiction. | Mothers and sons—Fiction. | Set theory—Fiction.
Classification: LCC PZ7.1.L4873 Be 2020 (print) | LCC PZ7.1.L4873 (ebook) | DDC [E]—dc23
LC record available at https://lccn.loc.gov/2019027461
LC ebook record available at https://lccn.loc.gov/2019027462

Illustrations done in digital media
Display type set in Paquita Pro by Juanjo Lopez
Text type set in Helenita Book by Rodrigo Araya Salas
Color separations by Colourscan Print Co Pte Ltd, Singapore
Printed by 1010 Printing International Limited in Huizhou, Guangdong, China
Production supervision by Brian G. Walker
Designed by Jon Simeon and Sarah Richards Taylor